Eavesdrop

When Terri hear[...] [...] the landing and le[...]

"Gosh, Vanessa, [...] [...] horrible," Berry said.

"I know. I hate to have to kill them. But what else can we do?" said Vanessa.

Kill? thought Terri. Kill what?

Terri was thunderstruck. She was listening to her stepsisters plotting a murder!

An absolutely terrible memory flashed through Terri's mind. It was a sentence from the letter Berry had written. *"We will have to get rid of the Turners . . ."* Stunned, she crept away from the door.

Watch for these other SCRAMBLED EGGS titles:

THE SISTER PLOT

By Suzanne Allen

Illustrated by Cornelius Van Wright and Ying-Hwa Hu

SPLASH™

A BERKLEY / SPLASH BOOK

SCRAMBLED EGGS #3, THE SISTER PLOT, is an original publication of The Berkley Publishing Group. This work has never appeared before in book form.

A Berkley Book/published by arrangement with General Licensing Company, Inc.

PRINTING HISTORY
Berkley edition/September 1990

ISBN: 0-425-12476-2
RL: 3.3

A BERKLEY BOOK® TM 757,375
Berkley Books are published by The Berkley Publishing Group, 200 Madison Avenue, New York, New York 10016. The name "BERKLEY" and the "B" logo are trademarks belonging to Berkley Publishing Corporation.

PRINTED IN THE UNITED STATES OF AMERICA

10 9 8 7 6 5 4 3 2 1

SCRAMBLED EGGS

THE SISTER PLOT

Chapter One

Beryllium Turner was writing in her diary. The words were very private. Some people use a secret code in their diary. Berry didn't need to use a code because hardly anybody on earth could read her handwriting.

> My dearest true twin sister Annamarie,
>   It is nine long years since we were separated at birth. I hardly remember what you look like. Are you still all pink and wrinkled? (Joke. Ho ho.)

Berry herself was pink and wrinkled, that was the real joke. She was writing as she lay in the bathtub. The water was getting cold, she'd been there so long.

Berry stopped writing for a moment. Her skin made rude scrunching noises on the bottom of the bath as she eased herself down the tub. Berry's foot touched the handle of the hot tap. She turned it expertly with her toes. Then she sighed with pleasure as hot, skin-wrinkling water flooded into the tub.

Berry felt perfectly private.

These days, it was hard to feel private in Berry's house. Not all that long ago, her name had been Beryllium Sterling. Her family had only been small—one mother, one brother and two sisters, five cats, six goldfish, and two turtles. Well, it was sort of small. Smaller than it was now, anyway.

Then Mrs. Sterling married Mr. Turner. The Turner family arrived to live in the rambling old Sterling house in San Diego. Suddenly Berry had an extra brother and two more sisters.

The Turners brought a pet with them, too. He was bigger than all thirteen Sterling pets combined. His name was Bart. He was an enormous Newfoundland dog, with black and white shaggy fur.

Bart Turner lived in the backyard in a beautiful little house of his own. Bart had two bad habits. He gobbled his food with a noise like a toilet plunger. And he shed long hair everywhere. But since Bart lived outdoors, nobody minded much.

Everyone *did* mind Berry's bad habit, which was hogging the bathroom. The only bathroom. But Berry was getting pretty good at ignoring fists hammering on the door and voices hollering from outside. She stewed and stewed in the warm water and wrote secrets to her long-lost true twin sister.

Annamarie, I think you will like our new stepsister Terri. She is only three days younger than us. That makes her an almost-triplet.

Of course, Terri is not as beautiful as you. And she does not have a brilliant imagination, like me. (She gets mad when I tell her this. Why? She can't be good at *everything*.)

But I wish I could trade places with her in *one* way. She gets things *done*. She keeps on pushing and pushing. If Terri was your long-lost twin sister instead of me, nothing would stop her. She would get to Paris, France, one way or another.

Annamarie, for your sake I am going to try to be just like Terri. I am going to push our whole family until we go to Paris for a holiday.

For two days, Bart had been limping just a little. Now it was five o'clock on Sunday afternoon. Up in the bathroom, Berry was slowly turning into a

3

large pink prune. Down in the den, Mr. Turner was examining Bart's paw.

"Come and have a look, everyone!" shouted Dorothea, their Australian housekeeper. "I've never seen anything as foolish in my life!"

Mr. Turner had collapsed into the big easy chair with Bart in his lap. The whole left side of Mr. Turner's face was covered in drool.

To be carried like a baby! To be inside the house! Both! At the same time! Bart just knew he had died and gone to dog heaven.

Bart understood right from wrong, but he couldn't resist. His huge, pink tongue crept slowly out of his mouth and slopped Mr. Turner on the ear. "Stop that, Bart!" commanded Mr. Turner. He used his fiercest army voice, but it was no use. Bart had never been in the army.

One by one, almost the entire huge family came to laugh at a dog the size of a small donkey being cradled like a baby.

Mrs. Turner's children (the former Sterlings) were all kind of sloppy and easygoing. They were happy to have Bart in the house, and secretly pleased to see dog-slobber all over their neat stepfather.

One by one, sixteen-year-old Vanessa, fourteen-

4

year-old Tristan, and twelve-year-old Isabella took turns tousling Bart.

"You look like a real goofball, Bart," said Izzy as she ruffled the hair on his head. It was true. His four feet pointed stiffly upward as though he was standing on the ceiling.

"Where's Berry? She should see this," said Vanessa, looking around.

"Haven't you tried to get into the bathroom for the last hour?" said Tristan.

Yes, Berry was still in the bath, humming the one special note that echoed off the tiles and made the bathroom window buzz loudly. Berry had not heard Dorothea's call.

When Mr. Turner's children (the true Turners) arrived in the den, both fifteen-year-old Paul and thirteen-year-old Melissa scolded their father. "You know how frightened he is of cats," said Paul. "You shouldn't bring him in the house," said Melissa.

But Paul and Melissa had grown up with Bart. They loved him as much or more than anybody. They took turns tousling Bart, too, even while they were complaining to their father.

"Terri! Come and tell Dad off, too!" shouted Paul at the ceiling. His father frowned. Paul blushed and apologized. He knew what he had done wrong. True Turners didn't bellow at ceilings. It was something that former Sterlings did.

Terri was lying on her bed upstairs in the tidy half of the room she shared with her stepsister, Berry. Faintly, Terri heard her brother's voice. She didn't move. Terri was much too busy to look at Bart.

Terri was busy worrying.

She supposed it was all her fault, really. She had started to say nasty things first. The reason for the argument was the usual one—the bedroom she shared with Berry.

It was unbelievable! After weeks and months, after dire warning from their parents, the two girls still shared a killer closet.

Oh, sure, it looked innocent enough with the door closed. But if anyone opened it without putting their hand in just the right place—*bonk, kabonk, crash!* Shoes kicked at stomachs. Dirty sweatshirts wrapped around ears. A toppling tower of junk buried people alive.

Berry preferred to lie on her bed and *talk* about organizing it. "Then we can put the games on the second shelf . . . or no, we'll put your books on that shelf . . . or no, I imagine maybe . . ." Berry would say. She wouldn't actually move a muscle to *do* anything.

Terri usually stood by the open closet door with her hands on her hips, fuming. An hour ago, Terri had finally blown up.

"I don't care *how* much you imagine!" said Terri. "Your imagination can't lift junk off the floor of the closet!"

"Yeah? Well, at least I *have* an imagination," Berry said. Then she stamped off to have a bath.

Berry had touched on a sore point with Terri. There were lots of things Terri didn't admire about Berry. Berry didn't know how to dress properly. She had freckles. She was a slob. And Berry always had trouble getting anything done.

But there were a couple of things about Berry that really impressed Terri. Berry always seemed to come up with the best ideas about, well, everything.

No doubt about it, Terri envied Berry's imagination. What's her secret? wondered Terri. She lay on the bed and stared at her carefully trimmed fingernails.

Berry bit her nails. Maybe that was it. Maybe nail-biting helped the imagination. Terri took an experimental nibble at a pinkie finger. Ugh. She hoped it was something else.

Downstairs, the dog-repair team was hard at work. "Stop jostling him, everybody, for goodness sake!" commanded Mrs. Turner. She was armed with tweezers. Dorothea stood beside her, holding up a table lamp.

"I thought so. There's a little thorn between his pads," said Mrs. Turner. "Hold still, you brave dog. We'll have it out in a second." Bart had never had so much attention in his life. His huge brown eyes were watering with happiness.

What a shame his happiness wasn't going to last!

That's because one more Turner decided to pay attention to Bart—Ratatooey Turner. Ratatooey Turner was orange and white, overweight, and a cat.

The Rat was sound asleep when something very heavy plumped down on the chair above his head. Then a whole forest of ankles crowded around in front of his sleepy eyes.

Curiosity overcame the Rat. He yawned, stretched, and backed out from under the arm-chair. The Rat crouched down and pumped his bot-

8

tom up and down a few times to oil his joints. Then he sprang directly up onto the back of the arm-chair.

The Rat was much wider than the chair top. He spilled over onto Mr. Turner's shoulder and sank his claws in to steady himself. At the same time he came nose to nose with Bart.

Mr. Turner screamed as the sharp claws dug into his shoulder.

The Rat popped liked a twenty-pound kernel of popcorn. One second he was a sleek fat cat. Then, kapuff! He opened like a beach umbrella. Suddenly he was twice as large—a cloud of fuzz that seemed to fill the sky in front of Bart's eyes.

Bart was terrified of cats. "Wowowowowow!" he roared. Everyone jumped back from the chair, holding their hands to their ears.

Bart had no time to scramble to his feet. Flat on his back, he began to run for his life. Naturally, he went nowhere. For a long moment the cat and dog remained nose to nose.

Mr. Turner had to do something, anything, to get the sharp claws out of his shoulder. But his arms were trapped under Bart. So he did the only thing he could. He heaved himself to his feet.

The Rat let go to avoid falling backward off the chair. Bart was dumped in a heap on the floor.

"Look out!"

"Ow!"

Bart's legs spun like windmills, bashing shins left and right. Then he was on his feet, crashing and bumping through the family toward the living-room door.

Chapter Two

Bart's nightmare was not over.

There in the hall was Fooey. Fooey was a black and white cat the size of a small laundry basket. She was minding her own business, staring at the front-door handle and waiting for somebody to let her out. Fooey did not even *see* Bart.

But Bart saw Fooey. His claws scrabbled on the hall floor as he changed directions. Only one direction looked safe to Bart—up. He shot up the stairs to the second floor.

Ralph, the oldest cat in the house, had also been sitting quietly, minding her own business, at the head of the stairs. Bart exploded onto the landing and trampled right over Ralph before he could stop himself.

There were no open doors on the landing, no way for Bart to escape. He stopped and turned. Now there was no way back downstairs. His way was blocked by the biggest cat in the family, the mother of all the other cats.

Ralph hated dogs as much as Bart hated cats,

even when they didn't treat her like a furry football and boot her all over the landing. She put her ears back, opened her mouth, and made a noise like a car tire spinning on ice.

"Bowowowow" barked Bart. Then he started to scramble backward.

The lock on the bathroom door was mostly for show. When Bart hit the door with his backside, the lock gave way.

Berry, half asleep in the lukewarm water, was stunned by the crash of the door hitting the toilet. Then wave after wave of wild woofing echoed off the tiles.

A second later something huge crashed backward into the bath, bringing down the shower curtain with it. Bart had backed up as far as he could go. There was only one direction left—down.

Bart loved water, particularly warm water. He loved warm water better than anything in the world next to being cradled like a baby. The tub seemed crowded to Bart. It was full of ripped plastic shower curtain. And something under the curtain was large and lumpy. That made it difficult for Bart to flatten himself right down in the tub.

Nevertheless, he tried his best. Bart hunkered down into the warm cozy water. And with his head below the edge of the tub he could no longer see the horrible cat-monster now sitting in the door-way to the bathroom.

Was Berry drowning or smothering? There was a great weight across her chest that made it difficult to breathe. Her ears were certainly under water. But her mouth might only be blocked by plastic shower curtain.

One thought pushed all others from her mind. She had to keep her diary dry! By enormous effort, she had managed to hold it out of the water. Now she strained to drop it over the edge of the bath.

With her other arm, she shoved at the heavy weight on top of her. That was a mistake. Bart shifted around, settling his body over Berry's head. Water flooded into her mouth. Now she really *was* drowning.

Terri was the first family member to reach the bathroom.

In the bathtub she saw only Bart tangled in the ruined shower curtain and—a book perched on the side of the bath.

"Bart! You fool!" she scolded. Terri leapt forward to save the book before it tumbled into the water. There was a ripping sound as she pulled it away from the edge of the bath.

And where the book had been, Terri saw a wrinkled hand hanging on tightly to a single sheet of paper. It was the hand of someone who had hogged the bath for too long, and was now paying a terrible price!

"Berry!" shrieked Terri. Terri dropped the diary and grabbed Berry's wrist.

For a moment, Terri seemed to have superhuman strength. She gave a single mighty pull. Berry shot right out from under Bart and the shower curtain to flop, coughing and gagging, on the bathroom floor.

"Are you all right, Berry?" said Terri anxiously.

Berry staggered to her feet and embraced her stepsister.

"Oh, Terri! You saved my life!" she said. Then she turned and looked down at the mess in the bath.

Bart was pleased that Berry was gone. There was much more room and he could submerge almost completely. Now only his eyes, nose, and the top of his head showed above the water.

He looked silly—a hairy, black bath-alligator with a short snout. Berry was not amused. "You dumb, dumb dog!" she shouted. "You almost killed me!" She gave a wild swing with her hand toward

15

Bart's bottom. All she did was splash water all over the bathroom.

"Thanks a *lot!*" complained Terri, jumping back.

"Ow! Ow!" said Berry. She had bruised her forearm on the side of the bath.

Bart's tail popped out of the water and wagged from side to side. *Slosh, slosh, slosh.*

"Are you all right, Berry?" It was Mr. Turner, heading a crowd at the doorway.

Terri turned. She saw all the faces and swung the door shut. "For heaven's sake, don't be so rude!" she shouted through the closed door. Berry was, after all, stark naked. Terri pulled a towel off the rack and handed it to her stepsister.

Berry smiled weakly and thanked her.

"You *are* all right, aren't you?" called her mother through the door.

"Yes, she's fine," said Terri. For the moment she had taken charge of her slightly older sister. Now she turned to scold Berry. "I don't know, Berry, sometimes I think you're—you're— What do they call people who always have accidents?"

"Accident-prone!" called Vanessa through the door.

"Go away! Give us a little privacy, can't you?" shouted Terri through the door.

Then she turned back to Berry, who was toweling herself off, and said, "Accident-prone. Exactly."

"Come on!" said Berry. "You can hardly call *that* my fault." They both turned and looked down at the brown soulful eyes of their very own bath-alligator.

Bart did not look too eager to move, but Terri reached down and grabbed him by the collar.

"Bowowowowow!" The two girls were nearly deafened by the barking. They had hardly noticed Ralph sitting under the sink, watching all the action.

"Oh, for heaven's sake!" said Terri. She caught Ralph around the middle, cracked open the door, and tossed the fat cat out. There was still a crowd goggling on the other side. Terri shut the door firmly in their faces, and soon they wandered off. It's not much fun crowding around a closed door.

While Terri soothed Bart and toweled up the slosh, Berry collected her diary off the damp floor and crept back to her bedroom. Soon Terri followed. Bart was left alone to calm down.

*　　*　　*

17

Half an hour later, Terri heard her name called from the bathroom. When she got there, she found Paul and Melissa. They were both wearing bathing suits. They looked wet and annoyed.

Bart had been given a bath. He loved water but hated soapsuds. He hated blow driers even more. Now he stood in the middle of the floor, shivering with misery, even though he was clean and dry and fluffy.

Bart looked hopefully at Terri. His eyebrows said, Take me out of this horrible place, please!

So Terri caught Bart by the collar and led him down the stairs. The entire household was glad to see him go.

Much to Terri's relief, they made it out the back door without seeing a cat. Outside, she clipped Bart's collar to the long leash that stretched across the backyard.

Bart didn't wait for her to finish. He had something on his mind. He hunched his back and bent over. Then he opened his mouth wide and went "Braak-acck."

Something white and slimy fell out of his mouth.

"Ick," said Terri, jumping back. At first she thought Bart was just making a sidewalk pizza, probably from swallowing too many soapsuds. But something caught her eye. There was a flicker of color in the disgusting little white pile under Bart's nose. What had he been eating that was blue? Had he gotten into the toothpaste?

She bent down and examined the mess more closely. Now she could see that it was a piece of paper. The blue color was ink.

Terri remembered seeing the torn diary page in Berry's wrinkled hand. Was this it? Terri was curious.

But was she *that* curious?

She was. Wrinkling her nose, she picked up the slimy blob between thumb and forefinger. She marched it over to the garden hose, where she washed it gently in fresh water. Then she spread out the paper.

Bart had chewed great holes in it. In spite of this, Terri recognized her stepsister's handwriting. Berry's handwriting was easy to recognize, but almost impossible to read.

Terri worked at it for a long time. It seemed to be addressed to . . . ? "My nearest turpentine banana tree"? Not likely. "My sneering glue fin and a bee"? That didn't make much sense, either.

She had it now. It was not a diary page after all, but a letter. It was addressed to "My dearest true twin Annamarie." Terri frowned. That hardly made any more sense than the other sentences. Berry didn't have a twin.

Terri kept working at the torn piece of paper. In the end, she deciphered several part sentences.

". . . now that my stepfather is making lots of money we can be together at last."

". . . we will have to get rid of the Turners . . ."

"I'll see you in a day or so, Annamarie. Let's meet at the . . . Tower . . ."

Terri sighed. Just like Berry to write a whole lot of silly nonsense to somebody who didn't exist. She screwed up the damp page into a little ball, went around the side of the house, and tossed it into a trash can.

Chapter Three

That night at bedtime, the air was strained in Berry and Terri's room. Both girls lay on their beds. Both girls were pretending to read.

Berry was thinking about how much she envied Terri. But she didn't say anything like that because Terri was being a pain in the neck.

Terri was thinking about how much she envied Berry. But she didn't say anything because Berry was being crabby.

So they both lay silently, each lost in her own little world. Berry was remembering how quickly Terri had pulled her from the tub. How Terri had taken charge, shooing everyone away, finding a towel for Berry, getting rid of the cat, cleaning up the flood in the bathroom.

That was just the kind of *doing* that Terri was so good at. And me, what about me? thought Berry. What was I doing? I was making a fool of myself, that's what.

Berry thought it would be all right to die jumping from the top of the Eiffel Tower in Paris and having your parachute fail to open. Being eaten by a shark while deep-sea diving was kind of classy, too.

But to be smothered to death in your bath by a wet dog? How embarrassing! How pathetic!

Berry almost felt like she'd like to tell Terri how much she admired her, and how foolish she felt drowning under Bart. Except that Terri had done too much nagging and telling Berry she needed a nanny.

Still, whether Terri knew it or not, Berry was determined to become a little more like her step-sister. Berry wanted to be somebody who Got Things Done. She fell asleep making plans. She was about to start pushing her family to Paris, France. And she would finish, too.

Terri, meanwhile, was thinking about the disaster in quite a different way. How does Berry always manage to make herself the center of attention? wondered Terri, with just a touch of admiration.

Terri had been brought up to be well mannered and polite. She was naturally graceful and did not trip over chairs at just the wrong moment. Terri was quiet, almost shy, in public. And what was the result?

Nobody ever notices me except when I'm with Berry, she thought. I'm dull. Not Berry.

Berry only has to put her lunch down on the ground for a second and a bus is sure to run over it. Tickle Berry day or night, and she was sure to have a mouthful of milk. Terri had even seen Berry get her teeth caught in another girl's hair. It was incredible, because Berry didn't wear braces!

Those kinds of things happened to Berry often. Terri knew that it wasn't just luck. Somehow Berry *made* little accidents happen. Accidents that made her the center of attention.

Well, Terri wasn't crazy enough to hang around under pigeons just to get more attention for herself. But Terri was sure there *was* one way she could be more like Berry, if she worked hard at it. Terri could show a little more imagination.

Take that soggy piece of paper that Bart had sicked up, for example. What would Berry have done with that? wondered Terri. Would she have just screwed it up and thrown it away?

No way! Berry would have gone all wide-eyed and breathless. She would pull all kinds of secrets and mysteries out of the few still-readable words.

And what did I do with it? Nothing. Well, I can fix that, decided Terri.

A few minutes later, a flashlight beam was probing deep into the trash cans beside the Turner house. Ick! said Terri to herself. Pawing through trash was not a job for a true Turner. At last she found it—a small, damp wad of paper.

Back up in her room, Terri climbed into her bed and listened to Berry's breathing. Yes, Berry was asleep. Terri turned off her bedside light. Then for once, Terri did what Berry always did. She pulled the covers over her head and turned on her flashlight.

". . . now that my stepfather is making lots of money we can be together at last."

". . . we will have to get rid of the Turners . . ."

"I'll see you in a day or so, Annamarie. Let's meet at the . . . Tower . . ."

Terri strained her imagination as hard as she could. For a very long while, she could only imagine her fruitcake stepsister, the freckled dwarf, scribbling nonsense in her diary and giggling to herself.

Then gradually, other ideas began to pop into Terri's head. Silly ideas. Dumb ideas. Just the kind of nonsense that Berry was always imagining.

Like bits of a jigsaw puzzle, Terri began to fit all the ideas together into one stupendously stupid idea. In the end, she had unlocked all the secrets of the letter. She knew just what the letter *really* meant.

Berry's true father, Mr. Sterling, had not died several years ago. He was still living somewhere in San Diego with Berry's true twin sister, Annamarie. Probably there were several other brothers and sisters, too. And pets, there had to be pets. There were lizards called Ernie and Bernie, and flying squirrels that knocked over lamps.

Berry's mother was just pretending to be Mrs. Turner until she got her hands on all the money that Terri's father was making with the new movie theaters he owned over in Prospect Park Mall. When that happened the Sterling half of the family would "get rid of" the true Turners. At this point Terri paused in her imaginings for a delicious shudder.

Then Berry would be reunited with her twin sister Annamarie at last. Meanwhile, they would meet secretly at the something Tower something.

It was all such nonsense! Terri, buried under her covers, suddenly laughed. Her voice sounded very loud in the silent bedroom. Berry, sleeping soundly in her nearby bed, rolled over, but did not awaken.

Chapter Four

As Terri dressed for school the next morning, she was still enjoying her wild imaginings of the night before. She chattered cheerfully all the way to school.

After school that day, however, Berry said something that made Terri think hard.

"Why don't you go home without me, Terri?" she said. "I think I'm going to walk over to the mall."

"Great. I'll come, too," said Terri.

Berry frowned slightly. There was no way she wanted to let Terri know what she was planning. Berry had to *do* this plan on her own, otherwise it wouldn't count. "No, that's all right. I'll go alone," she said.

Now Terri was really worried. Just the other day Berry had announced that she was never going to the mall again. "It just makes me spend money," she'd said. They'd gotten their allowance the day before and Berry was broke already. So whose fault is that? Terri had thought at the time.

So why did Berry suddenly want to go to the mall now? And by herself?

Terri's heart gave a sudden lurch. *"Let's meet at the . . . Tower . . ."*

That must mean Tower Drugs, over at the mall! Of course! Perhaps her imaginings weren't so wild after all!

"They don't like us wandering around by ourselves," Terri said. "I'll go with you."

"It's all right if we tell them," said Berry, meaning her parents.

"But, you *haven't* told them," insisted Terri.

"Well how can I? They're both at the *mall,"* said Berry, beginning to grow annoyed.

"I don't think that makes any diff—" began Terri, but Berry interrupted angrily.

"Look! I want to go by *myself,* understand? I *don't* need you to baby-sit me. In spite of what you think, I'm *not* accident-prone!"

Terri opened her mouth, changed her mind, and closed it again. Why insist? If Berry wanted to meet secretly with some Annamarie person, then she wouldn't want Terri hanging around.

"Okay," said Terri.

Berry was surprised that Terri gave up so easily.

"Oh. I'll see you later, then," she said, and started off down the street.

A moment later she looked around and saw Terri following her. Berry stopped. Terri stopped, too.

Berry stormed back to Terri, furious. "Stop following me!" she shouted.

Terri looked innocent. "I'm not following you. It just so happens I want to go to the mall, too."

"Ha!" said Berry.

"Well, I'm sure the mall is big enough for both of us," said Terri. "If you don't want me following you, let me walk in front."

That's how they got to the mall, with Terri walking in front. Even though she was a whole block ahead of Berry she could hear her stepsister quite clearly. Berry always stamped when she was mad.

Terri had barely entered the mall when the stamping behind her stopped. She looked back. Berry had sneaked away in another direction.

Terri smiled to herself. She didn't need to follow Berry. If her guess was right, Terri knew just where Berry would go for her secret meeting. Terri turned and headed for Tower Drugs.

Terri's guess was wrong. Berry had disappeared into the Worldwide Travel Agency, just a few

stores down from her mother's store, Books & Bears.

She came out after a few minutes carrying a large brown envelope and a white tube, all neatly rolled up. Then Berry went straight to tell her mother she was at the mall.

Mrs. Turner was curious about Berry's parcels. Her daughter just shrugged and said in a mysterious voice, "You'll find out soon enough." And then you'll all be on a plane to Paris, France, Berry added silently.

What happened to Terri? Neither Berry nor her mother saw Terri for the rest of the afternoon. Berry was especially pleased she had managed to sneak away from her nagging stepsister.

Terri, meanwhile, strolled up and down the drugstore aisles, certain that Berry would arrive sooner or later. Then she saw a girl almost her own age march boldly up to the lipstick samples.

Can I do that, too? wondered Terri. Why not! She joined the other girl at the mirror. About twenty shades of pink later, Terri looked at the clock! Five-fifty!

Chapter Five

"Go up and get Terri, please, Berry," said Mr. Turner, after everyone else had assembled for dinner.

"She's not in our room."

Mr. Turner looked puzzled. "Wasn't she with you?"

"No, I came home with Mom. I thought she must have come with you," said Berry, looking puzzled, too.

"Come?" Mr. Turner said. "From where?"

"From the mall," said Berry. "We went over there this afternoon, but she didn't want to hang around with me." That was almost what had happened anyway.

Mr. Turner looked at his watch, horrified. "She's wandering around at the mall, all by herself, at this hour?" he said. He began to lose his breath, as he always did when he got really anxious. Everyone looked from face to face. Mr. Turner wasn't the only one who looked worried.

Thank goodness, before Mr. Turner had a

chance to have a heart attack, or call the police, the front door slammed. A moment later, Terri raced into the room, muttering excuses, and sat down.

"Well!" said Mr. Turner, still trying to catch his breath. "Well! So nice to see you, Terri." She smiled at him. He didn't smile back.

Uh-oh! thought Terri. Big trouble. She was right.

"Nice to know that *my nine-year-old daughter has finally decided to stop hanging around the mall all alone where nobody knows where she is!*" he roared. Terry looked down at her plate. Everybody else looked innocently at the ceiling.

Mr. Turner had a lot to say on this subject. One by one he explained in great detail what a person was allowed to do, and where, and with whom, until what time. It made for very monotonous dinnertime talk.

"Wow! I really needed that, Terri!"

"Great mealtime conversations when you're here, Terri!"

"Thanks a lot, Terri!"

One by one, as the Turner kids left the table, they told Terri exactly what they thought of her.

Part of Terri felt embarrassed. She certainly hadn't behaved like a true Turner.

Another part of her was confused. She had guessed wrong about Berry and the mysterious Annamarie. This whole imagination thing was turning out to have a dangerous side to it!

And a very teeny part of Terri was pleased. She had certainly managed to make herself the center of attention! She had done exactly the kind of stupid thing that Berry was so good at.

Berry said nothing to Terri. She had more important things to think about. She was just about to take the first big step to convince the family to holiday in Paris, France.

The long white tube was a poster, a generous gift from the owner of the travel agency. It was already hidden under her bed. That was to be the second part of her plan.

The first part depended on the brown envelope. Berry pulled it out from between her mattresses and carried it down to the little sun-room that Mr. and Mrs. Turner used as an office.

Shutting the door behind her, Berry opened the envelope. Inside was a glossy brochure about holidays in Europe.

She thumbed from page to page, reading carefully, until she finally found the advertisement she was looking for:

Two fabulous weeks in Paris, France!
Your hotel overlooking the world-
famous Eiffel Tower!

Berry carefully tore the page out of the brochure. Then she slipped out into the hall and stopped by the door to the den. Good! Nobody was inside. She entered and approached the battered old coffee table that everyone put their feet on while watching TV.

Berry placed the page from the brochure neatly in the center of the table. Then she crept away, hopeful that somebody would soon notice it.

Somebody soon did, but unfortunately not the way Berry expected.

Only moments after Berry left, Vanessa and Paul wandered into the living room, deep in discussion about math.

"You've got to divide everything by x-squared," explained Vanessa. "Look . . ." She held a felt pen in her hand, looking left and right for a scrap of paper to write on.

She spotted Berry's brochure page with its torn edge, obviously a scrap. A moment later it was covered in huge black algebra squiggles. "See?" said Vanessa.

"No, not really," said Paul, frowning. "Can't you find a better piece of paper? Your math is all mixed up with the Eiffel Tower."

Vanessa sighed. She turned the paper over, hoping it was blank on the other side. But it wasn't. So Vanessa dropped it back on the coffee table and the two of them left the room.

Not long afterward, Mr. and Mrs. Turner arrived. Mr. Turner turned on the TV. Mrs. Turner put her feet up on the coffee table, right on top of the brochure. She noticed it, picked it up, and studied it for a moment. Then she passed it to her husband.

"You don't suppose this is a hint that we need a holiday, do you?" she said. Mr. Turner examined the page.

"Maybe," he said at last. "But which one of our kids wants to spend two weeks in Bulgaria?"

"Of all places!" said Mrs. Turner with a shrug.

Mr. Turner turned the page over, just in case he was looking at the wrong side. But, no, the other side had been scribbled over with pen.

* * *

Berry lay in the dark, waiting. At last she heard Terri starting to snore. Berry slipped under her covers, flashlight in hand, and began to write in her diary.

Ma chère Annamarie,

It won't be long now! A little while ago I peeked into the living room. My parents were looking at a page from a travel brochure! They are starting to think about a holiday! I'm actually DOING it, just like Terri would.

Terri was only pretending to snore. As soon as she saw the light go on beneath Berry's covers, Terri dived under her own. She turned on her flashlight and carefully unfolded the still-damp page from Berry's diary.

Terri was annoyed with herself for guessing wrong about the words in the letter. Once again she studied them carefully.

". . . now that my stepfather is making lots of money we can be together at last."

". . . we will have to get rid of the Turners . . ."

"I'll see you in a day or so, Annamarie. Let's meet at the . . . Tower . . ."

36

Tonight, that second line was bothering her. Why would Berry say such a thing, even if she was making it up? The more she thought about it, the more it worried her.

Terri had believed until now that she and her stepsister had been getting along quite well. In fact, that all the true Turners and the former Sterlings had been getting along quite well. Berry obviously felt differently.

Her ears caught the sound of Berry's flashlight clicking off. Terri flicked off her own flashlight and crawled out from under the covers.

She lay awake for a long while, thinking. The more she thought, the gloomier she got. Berry was still awake; Terri could tell by her breathing.

Terri wanted to say, "Berry, have I done something wrong? How come you don't like me?" She opened her mouth, but no words came out. A lump in her throat stopped them.

At last, she pulled a pillow over her head. Maybe I should stop trying to imagine what that letter means, she thought as she drifted off to sleep. It's only making me sad.

But now that Terri had started imagining things about the letter, she found it harder than she thought to stop. That night she had a nightmare.

She dreamed that Berry wouldn't let her in the door of their bedroom. When Terri finally forced her way inside, she found that everything she owned, even her bed, had been pushed out the window onto the front lawn. As she was leaning out to look at all her belongings scattered on the grass below, Terri felt Berry come up behind her and push her out the window, too.

Terri woke up screaming. Daylight was streaming through the window. She was in her own bed, and all her belongings were still neatly in place. What a relief! Terri hurried down to breakfast and found only Berry at the table.

Why was Berry wearing a pancake on her head? No, it wasn't a pancake, it was a beret. Even stranger, Berry's cheeks were rouged. She was wearing bright red lipstick.

"Allo Terree!" said Berry in a strange accent. Her arms flew everywhere, knocking dishes off the table. "Ow are eeyou? Ah am fine. Zee wedder in Paree is terrifeek."

It wasn't Berry at all. It was somebody who looked exactly like her!

Terri suddenly found herself back in bed, sitting

38

bolt upright, her heart pounding. It had all been a dream, even the waking up part!

Now she *really* was awake. The room was still dark so Terri checked her wristwatch. It was a little past two in the morning.

Why was she so excited? For a moment she couldn't recall the reason. Then it hit her! That strange Berry-like creature in her dream—Terri had seen her before!

Ten minutes later, Terri was sitting in the downstairs den. Only the loud wheezing of three sleeping cats broke the silence of the night. Terri had a piece of cake on a plate beside her. It was an excuse, in case anybody found her downstairs in the middle of the night.

She turned on the TV, slipped a videotape into the videocassette recorder, and began to watch.

Not long ago, Berry had secretly made this tape. She had very carefully hidden it. Terri had only found the tape by accident. Fortunately, Berry still kept it in the same place.

And there was Berry now, on the screen, talking toward the camera. She looked awkward, as she always did on videotape.

Almost at once, Terri knew she was on the right

track. Berry's first words sounded like "Masher Annamarie . . ."

Annamarie!

Terri had not remembered hearing the name. Now, she sat forward and watched closely. For a moment the picture went black. Then, there on the TV was a strange kid, looking almost exactly like Berry. She was talking with a funny accent about the weather in "Gay Paree."

The first time Terri ever saw this videotape she was sure this creature was just Berry playacting. Now she was not so sure. She watched the figure again, and again.

Unlike Berry, this person was very confident on camera. Her arms flew right and left as she talked. The more Terri studied her face, the more she realized that the eyes, the nose, and the mouth were almost, but not quite, like Berry's.

Finally, Terri was certain. This was not Berry at all. This was somebody called Annamarie!

Astounding! What a terrible secret the Sterlings had kept from the Turners! Berry had a true twin sister who lived somewhere else!

It was frightening to think about. If the Sterlings had kept secret about *that,* how many other, more horrible things were they hiding from the Turners?

Terri was lifting her piece of cake from the coffee table when she noticed the page from the travel brochure. She picked it up, and another mystery was solved.

There, half hidden by black felt pen squiggles, was a tall structure that she had seen many times before—the Eiffel Tower. It came to her in a flash. Tower! Not Tower Drugs! The Eiffel Tower, in Paris!

Annamarie lived in gay Paree, and gay Paree was Paris, France! Berry was planning to see her in a day or two, at the Eiffel Tower!

Now Terri frowned. But surely not. Surely that had to be wrong. Nobody in the family was planning to travel anywhere, were they? Least of all to Paris, France.

Or were they? As Terri looked more closely, she realized that she was looking at a page from a travel brochure, advertising a holiday in France! Come to think of it, hadn't her stepmother been alone in the den, reading this, when Terri had kissed her good night?

Terri removed the videotape and crept back upstairs, her mind in a turmoil.

Chapter Six

The next morning, Terri was still confused. She kept giving Berry strange glances as the two of them dressed. How could she possibly share a room with me, and not tell me about a twin sister, wondered Terri. Unless—unless I can't really trust the ideas I have in the middle of the night.

But without even really trying, Terri suddenly thought of a way to find out if Annamarie really existed. Because if she lived in Paris, there was only one way Berry could *see* her in a day or so. Berry could make a videotape, and send it to her twin. Then Annamarie could tape herself, and send it back.

Nonsense, she told herself firmly. She *had* to stop thinking like this! She was imagining ridiculous things.

That morning, Berry waited impatiently for Terri to go down to breakfast. When at last she was gone, Berry bent down and pulled the rolled-up poster out from under her bed. It was time for her next big push to Paris, France!

She unrolled the poster on her bed and stood back, considering it carefully. Where to put it so everyone could see it? Hmm.

Then suddenly she had a brainstorm. There was a way to put this poster in many places! Berry hugged herself with delight.

No doubt about it, she had a brilliant imagination! And if I can learn to actually *do* things as well as Terri does, I'll become President of the United States, she decided.

Berry arrived last at the breakfast table. "By the way," she announced as she poured milk onto her cereal. "Whose turn is it with the video camera?"

Terri dropped her spoon into her bowl with a loud clatter.

"Sorry," she muttered. Was it really happening? Was Berry getting ready to send a videotape to this Annamarie?

"Me," said Vanessa. She sounded grumpy. Vanessa was not at her best in the morning.

"Can I borrow it?"

"No."

"Just for a little while, Vanessa. Puh-leez!" begged Berry.

"Well . . ." Berry's oldest sister was silent for a moment. "Would you help me, then, with something I've got to do?"

"Sure," said Berry. "What?"

"I can't tell you here," said Vanessa, glancing at all the curious faces around the table. "It's a secret."

Berry hesitated, but at last she agreed. She needed that camera.

Terri, meanwhile, was now planning to stick to Berry like glue. If she thinks she can videotape herself and send it to a twin sister in France without me knowing, she's crazy, Terri said to herself.

Both girls took their lunch to school. At lunch hour, Terri thought Berry was somewhere around the schoolyard eating her lunch.

Terri thought wrong. Berry had carried her lunch all the way home.

As Berry closed the front door behind her, though, she felt a hand firmly grip her shoulder. It wasn't an unfriendly hand, but it was a hand that belonged to someone who would want an explanation of what Berry was doing home in the middle of the day.

"And what are you doing home, then?" Dorothea demanded in her funny accent. "My Austral-ian outback special sandwich wasn't good enough?" Dorothea prided herself on the truly ter-rific lunches she made for everyone to bring to school. She always gave them funny names that usually had to do with her homeland, even if it was just a regular old peanut butter and jelly sand-wich.

"It was great!" Berry told her, and meant it. Berry had liked it so much after her first nibble that she'd eaten the whole thing on her way home. "Um, can I have another? And, um, can I go up to my room for a little bit until it's ready? You don't have to come up and get me," she hurried on. "I mean, I know you're busy so I'll just come down for it, okay?"

Dorothea burst out laughing, something she often did. "Well, I can see you've something secret to do, probably writing in that diary of yours. I won't disturb you, and I will make you another sandwich. But just make sure you get back to school on time."

"Thanks, Dorothea! You're a pal!" Berry hol-lered as she raced upstairs. Dorothea shook her head and headed for the kitchen.

Once upstairs, Berry carefully pinned her travel

poster to the back of her bedroom door. Then she set up the video camera.

It was another one of Berry's incredibly clever ideas. She had collected all the movie videotapes that the family owned, and planned to videotape the poster right over the boring message at the beginning of each. Then there would be no way anyone could miss it!

Too bad Berry's plan couldn't work, even though she tried over and over again. For some reason, she couldn't record anything on the movie tapes. At last she gave up, and simply pinned up the poster where it could not be missed. That ended step two of her plan to push the family to Paris. Not quite as successful as she had hoped.

Still, such a setback would never stop Terri. It wasn't going to stop Berry, either. There was still a little time left before she had to be back at school, so Berry started on step three.

That meant leafing through a stack of old magazines in the sun-room office. As she leafed, she munched the second sandwich she had gotten from Dorothea. It was even better when you ate it sitting down, she thought. At last she found an advertisement she had noticed a few weeks ago.

MONDO VIDEO FILM CLUB
Join Now and Receive
the Following Fabulous Features!
Four Fantastic Foreign Films for only $4.44!

And yes, just as Berry had remembered, there was a whole column of French films to choose from. A couple of them even had "Paris" in the title!

Berry carefully cut the advertisement out of the magazine. Then, with only a few minutes left before the first afternoon bell rang at school, she ran out the front door and off down the street.

After school, Berry wanted to get on with her plans, but Terri was being a real pain again. At last, as Terri followed her upstairs for the fourth time, Berry could stand it no longer.

"Would you leave me alone! Stop breathing down my neck!" she shouted.

Terri finally left Berry alone in their bedroom. She sat across the hall on Melissa's bed, watching the closed door of her own bedroom.

With a sigh of relief, Berry opened her sock

drawer. She was going to need money for the next part of her plan.

In the back of the drawer she kept two little boxes. One was labeled *Petty Cash*. Berry opened it. Eight cents.

The other box was labeled *T.T.P.F.* Only Berry knew that it meant "Trip To Paris, France." Inside the box was Berry's precious travel fund. But when she opened the lid, there was a single white slip of paper in the box. It read: *I.O.U. $7.50, Beryllium Turner.*

Darn! She'd forgotten all about that neat Shark Attack T-shirt—the one all ripped and stained with fake blood along one side. She'd bought it last weekend at the mall.

On any day in the Turner family, only one person was *certain* to have money. Reluctantly, Berry opened the door to go find that person. She didn't have to look very far.

"Wanna buy my white teddy bear?" Berry asked Terri.

"What? The dirty one?" scoffed Terri.

"He's not *that* dirty," said Berry. "Besides, I'm desperate. I need to mail something."

Terry said nothing. Her mind was racing now. Mail what? It must be bigger than a letter. You could always find a stamp for a letter. Did Berry want to mail a videotape?

"Well, you want to buy Fluffy?" asked Berry again.

"Beryllium, I already *own* Fluffy," said Terri. "You sold him to me last month. You borrowed him again last week, remember?"

"So how about my stuffed turtle?" asked Berry.

Terri made a face. "Him? He's revolting. He's falling apart. What about your giraffe?" said Terri.

"I'll never, ever, ever sell George the Giraffe," said Berry. She swept up her very favorite stuffed toy and cuddled it.

"Four dollars," said Terri.

"Never!" said Berry. "Poor, poor Georgie," she crooned as she rocked George back and forth. "Anyway, I need five."

Terri thought hard. She wanted Berry to be able to mail that videotape. If she could get a good look at the address, she'd know for sure about Annamarie.

Was it worth five dollars to find out? Back in San Francisco, she had managed a paper route for nearly two years. Terri had quite a bit of money.

"Okay," Terri said at last. "Five dollars. But this is the *last* stuffed toy of yours I'm buying."

"Well . . . okay," said Berry. "As long as you promise I can buy George back when I have the money."

"Yeah, yeah," said Terri wearily. "Only his name isn't George anymore. I'm going to call him Gawky."

"Ugh," said Berry, as she kissed her pet and handed him to her stepsister in exchange for a five-dollar bill. Then she raced downstairs to do one last thing in order to join the Mondo Video and order her French videotapes.

Mrs. Turner was working at the desk in the little sun-room, her reading glasses perched on the tip of her nose.

"Mom, I'm going to buy some videotapes—"

"I'm not lending you any more money," said Mrs. Turner.

"I don't need any money," said Berry. "I just need somebody older than eighteen to sign the application form."

"Sign where?" said Mrs. Turner, hardly looking as Berry pushed the form under her nose. Berry's mother had been signing checks and paying bills all afternoon. She scribbled her name on the line beside Berry's finger, and that was that.

* * *

50

When Terri heard the front door bang, she raced to the window. There was Berry going down the front path. Terri had almost let Berry get away with the proof she had a twin sister.

"Terri, stop treating me like a baby. I can walk to the post office by myself," complained Berry when Terri caught up with her.

So, I was right! thought Terri. Then she said, "I'm doing you a favor. You heard what Dad said last night, Beryllium. You'd be crazy to walk around by yourself. For a week at least, anyway."

Berry sighed. Terri was probably right. "Well, I suppose you'd better come with me, then."

Terri had hoped to find a neatly wrapped video-tape in Berry's hands. But whatever Berry planned to mail was hidden in her knapsack. It could have been the size of a letter, a videotape, or even a small breadbasket.

Terri was cheerfully following Berry through the post-office doors when Berry stopped her. "I'm doing something private," she said. "You wait here, all right?"

"What? Don't you trust me?" said Terri angrily.

"I trust you," said Berry. "It's just private, that's all."

Terri sat outside on the steps and fumed.

To think that my own stepsister doesn't trust me! she thought to herself. She was also furious that she wouldn't get a peek at Berry's parcel.

In the end Berry caught Terri peering through the glass doors.

"You promised you weren't going to follow me inside," shouted Berry.

"What are you up to, anyway?" shouted Terri.

"Why are you sneaking around after me, anyway?" shouted Berry.

After a few more angry sentences the two girls stamped home in silence.

Berry was completely fed up with Terri. She was sick of the sight of her stepsister. When Terri sprawled on her bed after supper to do her homework, Berry collected hers and went down to do it on the front porch.

Terri, on the other hand, was furious that she had missed seeing Berry's parcel go into the mail. Now she would have to wait for a videotape to arrive from France to be certain that the mysterious Annamarie really existed.

And then, that evening, Terri overheard something that *really* made her worry.

*   *   *

Terri was just tidying her dresser top when she thought she heard Berry's footsteps on the stairs.

The footsteps started along the landing. Then Terri heard the sound of a bedroom door opening, followed by a voice.

"Don't forget you said you'd help me, Berry," said Vanessa.

The footsteps went into Vanessa's room. The door closed.

For a moment Terri was undecided. Like everyone else in the family, she had been curious about the "secret" Vanessa needed help with. Was she curious enough to actually snoop?

No, Terri wasn't quite that curious. But she was curious enough to just happen to be just passing close by Vanessa's door. And she was curious enough to be leaning toward the door, almost as if she were being dragged off her feet by a badly behaved dog.

When Terri heard her stepsister's voice she stopped on the landing, leaning like a tree in a strong wind.

"Gosh, Vanessa, it *is* kind of horrible," Berry said.

"I know. I hate to have to kill them. But what else can we do?" said Vanessa.

Kill? thought Terri. Kill what?

"How will you do it?" said Berry's voice.

"Well, I thought I'd use either chloroform or ether. Once upon a time they were both used to knock people unconscious when they needed a medical operation. But if you breathe enough of them, they'll kill you dead," said Vanessa.

"Ugh," said Berry.

Ugh is right! thought Terri. They're not actually talking about killing *people,* are they?

"It's not really 'ugh'," said Vanessa. "After all, we wouldn't want them to suffer. This way, they'll just go quietly to sleep and never wake up."

They? Who are *they?* wondered Terri.

"So, are we using ether or chloroform?" asked Berry

"Neither," said Vanessa. "I tried to get some at the drugstore, but they wanted an adult to come and sign for it."

"Why?"

"That way when somebody's murdered with ether or chloroform, the police can find out who bought it," said Vanessa.

Terri was thunderstruck. She was listening to her stepsisters plotting a murder!

"But, I've discovered something that works almost as well," said Vanessa. "Here, take a whiff."

"Eugh!" said Berry's voice. "It smells like a dry cleaner's!"

"Right. Perchloroethylene it's called. Dry-cleaning fluid. It'll kill them just as dead as ether," said Vanessa.

A faint smell of dry cleaning drifted out from under the door. Terri held her breath, just in case.

"So what do you want me for?" said Berry.

"I need another pair of hands," said Vanessa.

"Why not ask somebody bigger? Why not Mom?" said Berry.

"Come on! You know how squeamish she is!"

An absolutely terrible memory flashed through Terri's mind. It was a sentence from the letter that Berry had written. *"We will have to get rid of the Turners . . ."* Stunned, Terri tiptoed away.

For ages, she lay on her bed, staring at the ceiling, comparing that sentence to the conversation she had just heard. She didn't know what to think.

"We" meant Berry and who else? We will have to get rid of the Turners. Berry and Vanessa? When a call came from the bottom of the stairs, Terri didn't even hear it.

"Hey, does anybody want to see something strange in the den?" called Tristan.

One by one, everybody straggled into the den. All except Terri.

Tristan waited until they were all in the room. Then he closed the door. On the back of it was a poster advertising Paris, France.

"Who tacked that up?" said Mrs. Turner. Everybody shrugged. Nobody admitted it. Berry had no trouble shaking her head and saying that, no, she had not done it either. After all, you could easily see that the poster was not tacked up at all, but taped to the door.

"Did you put up the poster in the den?" Vanessa shouted up the stairs at Terri. Terri had no idea what she was talking about.

Incredible. Amazing. Everyone agreed.

"But what does it mean?" said Izzy.

"It means 'It's the life! In Paris!'" said Mr. Turner.

"But what does *that* mean?" complained Izzy.

Berry knew the answer. It meant that the whole family was standing around thinking about Paris! She was delighted. The poster had worked better than she had thought.

*   *   *

A little later Mrs. Turner drew her husband aside in the kitchen. "You don't suppose that was *another* hint about a holiday?" she asked.

He shrugged. "Could be," he said.

When Berry got back upstairs, she was surprised to find Terri already in bed, a pillow over her head.

Terri, for the first time in days, was trying not to imagine *anything*. But now that she had started, she just couldn't stop. She thrashed about in the bed, putting the pillow first over one ear, and then the other.

Berry, reading in the other bed, frowned over at Terri and wondered what was going on. Maybe her stepsister was coming down with something. Terri had been looking a little pale lately.

Chapter Seven

It was Saturday morning, a good morning to find somebody for a serious talk. That's what Terri had at last decided to do.

What about her father? Terri knew exactly what would happen if she told him about her fears. "Complete nonsense!" he would say.

Maybe it *was* complete nonsense. Terri certainly hoped so. But she was certain her father would say exactly the same thing whether it was nonsense *or not*.

Terri watched the cable news channel a lot. She knew that people did weird things every day. People suddenly murdered other people. It happened all the time. It could happen in San Diego. It could happen in the Sterling house, to the Turners.

Her father wouldn't believe it, no matter what, though. Terri just knew it.

No, the best person to talk to was Dorothea. She was sensible. She was trustworthy. She would surely be able to help Terri.

Terri knew where to find Dorothea on a Saturday morning—in her little room above the garage. Dorothea was really a folk singer, not a house-keeper. Folk singers stayed up late on Friday nights and took Saturday mornings off.

Terri crept up the stairs on the side of the garage, prepared to wake Dorothea up if necessary.

She had her hand raised to knock on Dorothea's door when she heard a voice. It wasn't Dorothea speaking. It was her stepmother!

"Travel arrangements are such a nuisance," said Mrs. Turner. "I'd help you if I could, but one of my staff is sick today."

"No problem," said Dorothea.

"Now it's *critical* that the Turners don't find out about this. Well, I mean, we're all Turners, but—"

"Leave it to me, Mrs. T.," said Dorothea. "I know what you mean."

So did Terri! Her stepmother meant the true Turners—Terri, her father, Paul, and Melissa. They weren't meant to know . . . what?

Now Terri heard the sound of footsteps in the room. She tiptoed down the steps as fast as she could and scampered around the corner of the garage, still dazed by what she had heard.

Terri took Bart for a walk around the block and tried to sort out her thoughts.

The Sterling half of the family were going to be traveling somewhere. But where? Terri hated to think about it, because, crazy as it seemed, the same answer kept popping into her mind.

After murdering the Turners, the Sterlings would all escape to Paris, where Berry would be reunited with her twin sister.

Well, whatever was going on, Mrs. Turner was in on it, decided Terri. And Dorothea, too.

What now? Tell her father? More and more it seemed the only sensible answer. But Terri desperately needed some kind of proof if she wanted him to believe her.

As the weekend wore on, Terri felt more and more that the proof was there, all around her. Vanessa had changed! She had always been the cheeriest member of the whole family. Now she became the creepiest.

Vanessa began to hang around everywhere, spying on Terri. Whenever Terri looked at her, Vanessa quickly pretended to be interested in a crack in the wall, or the ceiling, or something.

Terri grew more and more nervous. She moved from room to room. Sooner or later, she would look up, and there Vanessa would be behind her, studying nothing. It was scary.

Berry was everywhere, too, all weekend. But she was just annoying. She got in everybody's way, and most of the time she sounded like a broken record.

Over and over again, Berry sang some dumb song about Paris in the springtime, until everybody in the house was ready to scream at her.

For Terri, it was one more clue that the Sterlings would escape to Paris after "getting rid of" the Turners. But it wasn't until Monday that at last Terri saw a chance to get the proof she needed for her father.

Chapter Eight

On Monday morning, almost the entire Turner family had the Monday Morning Blues.

Berry had planned to wait until after step three (the French videotapes) before actually *mentioning* a holiday in Paris, France. When she saw all the gloomy faces at breakfast, she knew she had to say something.

"I think we all need a holiday. Pass the butter please," said Berry.

"You sound very old and wise this morning, Berry," said Mrs. Turner. "But, you know, I think you're right."

"I think Terri especially needs a holiday," said Paul, studying the youngest Turner with a serious expression on his face.

"Have you been sleeping properly, Terri?" said Mrs. Turner. Now that Paul mentioned it, she saw that her young stepdaughter did have bags under her eyes.

"I'm all right," said Terri. But she wasn't.

Unlike all the rest of the kids, Terri was looking

forward to getting to school. Right now she would do anything to escape the house. Especially that creepy Vanessa.

Terri looked up and saw Vanessa watching her, a warm, caring smile on her face. Terri didn't smile back.

There were some things you could learn from horror movies. Particularly the ones you weren't allowed to watch. In them, the nastiest ghouls behaved just like Vanessa. At first, you believed they were the sweetest, the nicest, the warmest people in the entire world. And then came that moment late at night when you found yourself alone in the house with them. Terri shuddered.

That afternoon when they got home, there was good news waiting for both girls. They passed Dorothea on the front walk. She was on her way to the little mall at the corner of the street.

"Oh, Berry," said Dorothea. "Check on the dining-room table. There's mail for you. It looks like a videotape."

"Yippee!" shouted Berry.

Terri was pleased, too, although she didn't show it. Here at last was her chance to get her hands on proof—a videotape of Annamarie from Paris.

Terri knew she had to wait to find the new video-tape of Annamarie until Berry had hidden it. So she did not follow Berry straight upstairs to her room. Instead, she spread her homework out on the dining-room table and began to work.

Best to give Berry a chance to hide the videotape in their shared bedroom, where Berry still hid everything. Terri knew she could find it.

Much to Terri's delight, her chance came more quickly than she expected—right after supper, that evening.

Berry was so excited! She waited in the den for the family to gather. This was going to get the entire family wanting to be in Paris, France, she just knew it.

Tomorrow, she would be able to pop the big question. "Hey, I was just thinking. Why don't *we* all go to Paris?" she would say. She had rehearsed the question over and over in her mind. She wanted it to sound perfect—as if she'd only just thought of it herself.

Tristan and Melissa were first to arrive. Out in the hall, Berry heard her mother calling up the stairs, "Terri! Berry has organized some kind of treat for us."

"Sorry, Mom. I've got a lot of homework," Terri called down. Quietly she eased the bedroom door closed and began to hunt for the videotape.

At that very moment, Berry was standing proudly in front of her family with two videotapes in her hand. Suddenly she felt self-conscious.

"Well, um, er. See, I joined this special video club and they've already sent me two videos, and there are two more coming," she mumbled. "And, like, I wanted you to see them, too, because they're so great!"

"Hooray! Movies!" There was cheering and clapping. Everybody in the family loved movies—at the cinema, or on videotape.

Berry slid the first videotape into the machine. The first picture that appeared on the screen was the famous half-smiling lady, the Mona Lisa. Over it, a title appeared: "The Art Treasures of the Louvre in Paris."

Almost at once, the audience became restless.

"This *is* a movie, isn't it?" said Izzy.

"I think so. Now shut up," said Berry. She had chosen the videotape from a list only because it had "Paris" in the title.

Painting after painting faded onto the screen. Then the camera dragged slowly from corner to corner of the painting, while the narrator droned on and on, telling the Turner family more than any of them had ever wanted to know about one of the world's greatest art museums, the Louvre.

"*Very* nice, dear," said Mrs. Turner at last. "What's the other videotape?"

"Yeah! What's the other one? We want the other one! We want the other one," chanted all the Turners. Berry, fuming, put on the second videotape.

This one wasn't as successful as Berry hoped, either. "Berry, fix the color! We can only see black and white," commanded Tristan.

Berry tried to fix the color, but there wasn't any. It was black and white.

"Why are there little sentences across the bottom of the screen?"

"When are they going to stop jabbering a foreign language and speak in English?"

The film was in French, with English subtitles.

Soon, Mrs. Turner fell asleep. Mr. Turner followed. Then Dorothea suddenly remembered she had a singing audition downtown. Soon Berry was all alone with her snoring parents.

Finally, Berry stormed upstairs.

*　　*　　*

Up in the bedroom, Terri was not having a good evening, either. She had practically taken the room apart, piece by piece. She could *not* find the new videotape from Annamarie anywhere.

Thanks to Berry's angry stamping on the stairs, Terri had lots of time to throw herself on her bed before the door banged open. Without a word, Berry threw herself on her own bed, arms crossed, and stared at the ceiling.

It was another evening in which neither Berry nor Terri had a word to say to each other. They both undressed silently and went to bed. Both girls fell asleep almost immediately. They were exhausted.

Chapter Nine

Berry and Terri overslept.

Both girls were horrified to find the dining room empty when they got down for breakfast.

"Better hurry, you two!" called Dorothea from the kitchen.

"Where is everybody?" said Berry.

"They're all gone!" called Dorothea.

Berry was disappointed. Even though the foreign film club was a disaster, Berry hadn't given up. She had planned to pop the big question this morning. But this morning there was nobody to pop questions to.

Terri was a little disappointed, too. Last night Terry had planned to confide her suspicions to her father. Even if he didn't believe her, Terri knew she would feel better talking to him. This plot by her sisters was starting to drive her crazy. "What about my father?" she called to Dorothea, just in case.

"Gone!" shouted Dorothea. "Everyone but you two." As it turned out, Dorothea was wrong.

At that moment they heard the sound of feet on the stairs. The smiling face of Vanessa poked through the dining-room door.

"Berry, could I see you for a minute?" said Vanessa. Terri slumped into her chair, feeling sick. Berry got up from the table and left the room.

Terri had been dreading the moment she saw Berry and Vanessa together again. She *had* to know what they were talking about. Terri got up and went to stand by the dining-room door. Now she could easily hear the whispering in the hall.

"How about this evening?" Vanessa said.

"Who do we get first?" said Berry.

"We'll sneak up on them one by one," Vanessa said. "We'll start with Bart. He'll be the easiest, I think."

"You've got the stuff?" asked Berry.

"Of course," Vanessa said. "We can't kill them without it!"

Terri was sitting at the table as white as a ghost when Berry came back into the room. What a fool she'd been, thinking that the Sterlings were nice people! Only the worst kind of monsters would kill a harmless dog, who'd never done anything to hurt them.

"Are you all right?" said Berry.

"What do you care?" snarled Terri. "No. I'm not going to school today!" Terri rushed out of the room. She had to get to her father as soon as possible and tell him everything.

But Terri hadn't reckoned with Dorothea. "Staying home is one thing. Wandering off to the mall is another," said Dorothea, her hand on Terri's forehead. "If you're sick to your stomach, hop into bed and stay there."

"But—" said Terri.

"Your father said he'd be home after lunch today. You can talk to him then," Dorothea said.

So Terri settled down into her bed to wait. Hour after hour dragged by. One o'clock came and went. Then two. Then three.

Terri went downstairs. "You said he was coming home after lunch!" she accused Dorothea.

Dorothea shrugged. "I said it, and so did he. Something must have held him up. You go on back to bed, now, and be patient."

Terri did, and promptly fell asleep. When she woke up it was four-thirty and her father was sitting on the edge of her bed, his hand on her forehead.

"Oh, Dad! I'm so glad to see you!" she cried, hug-

71

ging him tightly. "Something terrible is going to happen!"

They sat on the bed together, Mr. Turner holding Terri's hands. As Terri explained, his eyes grew wider and wider.

"You don't know everything about the Sterlings. You think you do, but you don't," said Terri. "I've found out some stuff. Scary stuff."

"Like what?"

"Like Berry has a real twin sister who lives in Paris, France."

"Terri, that's complete nonsense!"

"I *knew* you'd say that. But I can prove it to you!" said Terri. "I found a videotape Berry hid."

"What? How much peeking and prying into Berry's things have you been doing, anyway?" he said.

"Dad! It looks like Berry on the videotape, but it's not! I'm certain!" said Terri.

"This is absurd!" Mr. Turner said, shaking his head.

"Dad, there's more. I overheard Berry and Vanessa planning something terrible. Mrs. Turner knows about it, too. She told Dorothea especially not to tell us. The real Turners."

"What *have* you been doing, Terri? Listening at doors, too?" said Mr. Turner.

"I had to," said Terri. She lowered her voice to a whisper. "They're planning to kill us all," she said.

"*Who* is?"

"Vanessa. Berry's going to help her. They're going to use dry-cleaning fluid," said Terri.

"Terri, have you gone completely mad?" said Mr. Turner, astonished.

"I first found out about it when I read about it in a letter Berry wrote," said Terri.

Mr. Turner frowned. "You've been listening at doors, snooping, *and* reading your stepsister's letters?" he said.

"Dad!" said Terri. "This morning I heard them say they were going to start doing it this evening so I—"

Terri broke off. A single "wuff" echoed through the house.

Mr. Turner turned, looking puzzled. "That was Bart. What's he doing inside the house?"

Suddenly Terri stood and let out a shriek. "Oh, no! They've started already! They're killing Bart!" Before her father could stop her, she dashed out of the room.

73

"Terri! Wait!" he cried, running after her. Downstairs he found Terri pounding on the closed door of the living room.

"Let me in!" she shouted.

"Sorry, nobody's allowed in right now!" called Vanessa. Terri pushed at the door, but something was blocking it.

"Oh, no!" moaned Terri.

Her father put his hand on her shoulder. "Terri!"

But Terri was sniffing the air. Mr. Turner sniffed, too. The smell was unmistakable. Dry-cleaning fluid.

"They said they'd get Bart first! The window!" shouted Terri. And before her father could stop her, she shot out the front door and around the side of the house.

What she saw through the window of the living room was her worst nightmare come true.

Vanessa and Berry were hunched over the body of Bart, who had collapsed on his side.

"No!" shrieked Terri. It was like a scene from a horror movie.

"Oh, Dad! Dad! They're killing him! Please make them stop!" shouted Terri as her father came running up.

Mr. Turner reached in and pushed up the window from the outside.

"What on earth is going on in here?" he said. "And what is Bart doing in the house?"

At the sound of his name, Bart lifted up his head and wagged his tail.

Terri almost fainted from relief. "We're not too late! Come on, Dad!" And she scrambled in the window.

"Terri!" said the shocked Mr. Turner. He wasn't the kind of man who climbed through windows. But after a second, he shrugged and hoisted himself into the living room.

Terri, meanwhile, was trying to push Vanessa and Berry away from Bart. "Leave him alone, you monsters!"

"Settle down, Terri," said Mr. Turner, catching his youngest daughter by the shoulders. He turned to Vanessa and Berry. "Now, would somebody explain just what is going on in here?" he said.

Vanessa looked at Berry. Berry looked at Vanessa. Vanessa shrugged.

"We're looking for fleas on Bart," said Berry.

"And any other bugs we can find," Vanessa said. "We're going to do the cats, next."

"We've already caught two different kinds of ant

in his hair. Want to see?" said Berry. She lifted the lid of a plastic food container. Out wafted the powerful smell of dry-cleaning fluid.

At that moment, Terri shifted the chair that had been blocking the door. The room was suddenly crowded with anxious family members who had come running to investigate the commotion.

"What *is* all the fuss about?" said Mrs. Turner. "What's going on?"

Vanessa looked a little bewildered. "Well, I don't know what the fuss is about. But I can tell you what is going on," she said.

"Please," said Mr. Turner.

With every word Vanessa spoke, Terri felt more and more stupid. "I'm doing a science project. On insects," said Vanessa. "I'm calling it 'Jeepers Creepers.' I've been collecting all the different kinds of insects that live in the house with us."

"I'm sure we have hardly any," said Mr. Turner with a slight frown.

"Don't believe it!" said Vanessa. "It's incredible all the little creepy crawlies I've found, just by looking in cracks and corners. Ask Terri. She was following me around all weekend."

"No, *you* were following *me* around," said Terri. But suddenly Terri began to see Vanessa's behavior in an entirely new light. Suppose Vanessa had *really* been looking at the floor, and the ceiling, instead of just pretending to?

Meanwhile, Vanessa was showing the family the sheet of cardboard where she was mounting the insects. "Oh, my God! That's a cockroach!" said Mrs. Turner.

"Relax, Mom. It came in with a box of groceries," said Vanessa. "I think I got it before it laid any eggs."

"Hey, neat! This says 'Hair Louse,'" said Tristan, who was bending over, reading labels under the tiny insects.

"Lice? We have lice?" shrieked Mr. Turner, looking horrified.

"And bedbugs, too," said Tristan, still reading.

"Oh, my God! This is serious!" said Mrs. Turner, looking even more horrified than her husband.

Vanessa laughed. "The whole class went to the university for a visit to the insect department. They gave us free samples. I got the bedbug and the louse there."

"But, Vanessa! You certainly can't put them on your display as if they came from *our* house!" said Mr. Turner angrily.

"You don't want people to think *we* have bed-bugs, do you?" said Mrs. Turner, just as angry.

Vanessa sighed and looked at Berry. "See! *Now* do you understand why I was keeping it all a secret?" she said.

Meanwhile, Terri was sitting in a chair by herself. Bart's head was in her lap. She was feeling terribly relieved, and terribly foolish. She had just imagined everything, after all.

But then why had Mrs. Turner told Dorothea to keep a secret from Terri, and all the true Turners?

"Since everybody's here together, this might be a good time to make a little announcement," said Mrs. Turner.

She looked at her husband. He nodded.

"A few days ago, somebody left a page from a travel brochure around—" she began.

Berry's heart leapt. "I knew you'd see it!" she cried, interrupting her mother.

Mrs. Turner turned to Berry, a puzzled frown on her face. "So it was *you*, Berry. But why on earth did you want to go to Bulgaria?"

Suddenly, just as Berry's dream was coming true, it shattered. "Oh, no!" she cried. "There's been a terrible mistake! We *can't* go to Bulgaria!"

Mr. and Mrs. Turner both laughed. "Relax, Berry. We're not going to Bulgaria."

Berry sat down, weak with relief.

"Actually, we're going to Disneyland," said Mrs. Turner with a big beam.

"But—but . . ." spluttered Berry. She wanted to say, "But Disneyland's just up the road. Let's go someplace exotic—like Paris, France!"

"I wish we had enough money to go farther away," said Mrs. Turner with a small smile. "But we do have enough to stay at a motel and spend two full days at Disneyland."

She glanced at Berry and saw the expression on her face. "Berry, come on! Don't look so crushed. Some of us have never been to Disneyland before, you know," she said.

It was true. All the former Sterlings had been to Disneyland more than once. It *was* just up the road, when you lived in San Diego. But the former Sterlings looked at the true Turners and saw the delighted expressions on their faces. None of the true Turners had ever been to Disneyland.

The former Sterlings all suddenly realized that Disneyland would still be fun. More fun than ever, in fact, as they introduced their stepbrothers and -sisters to all the exciting rides.

Berry forgot all about Paris, France. She loved Disneyland.

Terri was so excited, she forgot all about everything. It was a wonderful relief. She felt as if she had been worrying for years.

Chapter Ten

Mrs. Turner drew Berry into the kitchen and closed the door. They were alone. Mrs. Turner looked stern.

"Berry, did you read the advertisement for the video club carefully before you joined it?" she asked.

"Sure. Four movies for four forty-four," said Berry.

"Did you read it *all?*"

"Sure."

"Well, I've read it now. You realize that over the next year you have to buy four more movies at twenty-nine ninety-five each?"

"Unh . . . I do?"

"You agreed to it when you signed the membership application," said Mrs. Turner.

"Well . . . unh . . . really, *you* signed it," said Berry.

"Oh, no! Don't even *think* it!" said Mrs. Turner firmly. "*You* belong to the club. *You* pay for the movies."

                    *   *   *

Mr. Turner drew Terri into his bedroom upstairs and closed the door. They were alone. He
looked stern.

"Terri, I'm concerned about what I've heard
from you today," he said. "I want no more creeping
and peeping and listening about the house."

Terri hung her head and nodded.

"I always thought your sister Berry had a wild
imagination," said Mr. Turner. "But she isn't even
in the same *league* as you."

"Really?" said Terri.

"Really," said Mr. Turner. "If they had a school
for wacko imaginations, Berry would be in kinder-
garten, and you would be in your final year of col-
lege!"

Mr. Turner was astonished when Terri suddenly
jumped up and gave him a tremendous hug. "Oh,
Dad! You say the nicest things!" said Terri. Then
she turned and ran to the door.

"Wait! I'm not finished!" called Mr. Turner.

But Terri was already out the door. "Don't
worry, Dad," she shouted. "I don't *have* to use my
imagination!"

And indeed, now that Terri knew she could

imagine things just as well as Berry, she wasn't
sure if she'd ever use it again.

You could get carried away with your imagination if you weren't careful. It was no fun, worrying
yourself to death. Terri was happy to leave that
to Berry, in the future.

Bart was in the backyard, lying up against his
doghouse. Berry was lying on the grass, her head
on Bart, gazing up at the evening sky.

She was feeling quite pleased with herself. She
had actually *done* something, just like Terri might
have done it. She had pushed and prodded. Because of it, her whole family would be going for a
little holiday next weekend.

The trouble was, it had been *such* an effort. The
last time they had gone to Disneyland it had
worked like this:

"Mom, could we go to Disneyland?" Berry had
said.

"Sure," her mother had said.

That was the best way to get things done. No
pushing. Now that she knew she could do it herself, Berry thought she might just let Terri do all
the hard work of actually pushing for things.

* * *

Terri found Berry in the backyard. She lay down beside her stepsister with her head on Bart. Two girls had their heads on him! At the same time! Bart was in dog heaven.

"Sorry about reading your diary," said Terri.

"That's okay," said Berry. "If Bart sicked it up, how could you know?"

"About this Annamarie—" said Terri.

"I don't want to talk about it," said Berry firmly.

They were silent for a moment. "I only want to know, why would you say you wanted to get rid of the Turners, anyway?"

Berry glanced around. Terri's lip seemed to be quivering. Berry sighed. "That's what you get for reading somebody's diary," she said. "I don't want to get rid of you. I like you. I was writing that I wanted to get rid of the Turners' *name.*"

"But why?"

"I just thought there might be something more interesting," she said. Like Annamarie's name, perhaps. Suddenly something occurred to Berry. She didn't know Annamarie's last name!

Ma chère Annamarie,

What a booboo! I have never learned your last name! I cannot imagine how these letters have been getting to you so well. Please write as soon as possible and let me know what it is. I just know it's beautiful!

Sorry I can't make it to Paris. I'll send you a postcard from Disneyland.

Your true twin, and almost step-triplet,

Beryllium

P.S. You wouldn't like to buy some video-tapes, would you? You'll love them. They're in French! Only $29.95 each. Plus tax.

It's where everything happens!
by Ann Hodgman

___#1: NIGHT OF A THOUSAND PIZZAS 0-425-12091-0/$2.75

It all started with the school lunchroom's brand new, computerized pizza maker. Instead of one-hundred pizzas, the cook accidentally programmed it to make one thousand! What can the kids do? Have you ever tried to get rid of a thousand extra-large pizzas?

___#2: FROG PUNCH 0-425-12092-9/$2.75

This time the principal has gone too far. Ballroom dancing lessons. UGH! Even worse, he's planned a formal dance. Now the sixth grade is determined to fight back. When they unleash their secret weapon in the lunchroom, things will go completely bonkers!

___#3: THE COOKIE CAPER 0-425-12132-1/$2.75

The kids want to sell their baked cookies to raise money for the class treasury. But where will they find a kitchen big enough? The lunchroom! The cookies turn out to be so amazing the kids at Hollis get to be on TV, but the baking business turns out to be more than *anybody* needed!

___#4: THE FRENCH FRY ALIENS
0-425-12170-4/$2.75

It's going to be super scary when the kids give their performance of the class play. Especially since the sixth grade's all-new *Peter Pan* looks like it may turn into The French Fry Aliens—an interplanetary mess!

295

One day Allie, Rosie, Becky and Julie saved a birthday party from becoming a complete disaster. The next day, the four best friends are running their own business...

Don't miss these Party Line Adventures!

by Carrie Austen

___#1: ALLIE'S WILD SURPRISE 0-425-12047-3/$2.75

Allie's favorite rock star is in town, but how will she get the money for a concert ticket? When the clown hired for her little brother's birthday party is a no-show, Allie finds her miracle! Before you can say "make a wish," the girls are in the party business--having fun and getting paid for it! Can The Party Line make Allie's rock concert a dream come true?

___#2: JULIE'S BOY PROBLEM 0-425-12048-1/$2.75

It's hard to get a romance going with the cute Mark Harris when his best friend, Casey Wyatt, is an obnoxious girl-hater. Then, in the misunderstanding of the century, The Party Line gets hired to give a party for Casey. When Casey finds out, it's all-out war.

___#3: BECKY'S SUPER SECRET   0-425-12131-3/$2.75

Becky is putting together a top secret mystery party and she'll need her three best friends to help her do it in style. The only problem is: Becky hasn't exactly told them yet that they're going to help. Can Becky pull off the surprise party of the year?

___#4: ROSIE'S POPULARITY PLAN   0-425-12169-0/$2.75

It's just Rosie's luck to get paired with Jennifer--the weird new girl--for an English project. Next, Jennifer's mom thinks it would be a great idea if The Party Line threw a birthday party for Jennifer. The rest of the girls will need some serious convincing!